THE ARROW THAT FLIES BY DAY

JOHN SERVANT

WESTBOW
P R E S S®
A DIVISION OF THOMAS NELSON
& ZONDERVAN

WestBow Press books may be ordered through booksellers or by contacting:

WestBow Press
A Division of Thomas Nelson & Zondervan
1663 Liberty Drive
Bloomington, IN 47403
www.westbowpress.com
1 (866) 928-1240

ISBN: 978-1-9736-0138-8 (sc)
ISBN: 978-1-9736-0137-1 (e)

Library of Congress Control Number: 2017913614

Print information available on the last page.

WestBow Press rev. date: 01/18/2018

A.M.D.G.

"You shall not fear the terror of the night nor the arrow that flies by day."

Psalm 91:5 NABRE

1

THE BEGINNING

He was about six feet two inches tall. He was slender but not overly thin, and he did not wear glasses. He appeared to be well-built. His pants were khaki and slightly wrinkled. His hair was brown in a crew cut, his complexion was ruddy, and his eyes were blue. He carried an old-looking brown leather jacket that had seen much wear but was not dirty. It was the kind of wear inflicted by someone who had only one jacket. It was warm, so he carried it. He wore an easy smile. He had an air of mystery about him, and he was certainly out of place where he was.

He had wandered onto the New Jersey Raptors' practice field on the first day of training camp. He'd come on foot. He had no car—just a knapsack. He had walked, but who knew from where? The athletes competing for spots on the team were already on the field. They were not in full uniform but in gray T-shirts and shorts.

He tried to approach the head coach, but his path was cut off by an assistant coach. "I'm sorry," the man said. "This is football practice. It is closed to the public."

"No worries, sir. I'm here to try out for the team."

The assistant coach smiled. "I'm sorry, young man, but all our draft choices and free agents are already here. We don't have any openings."

This was the safe response, since nothing in this young man recommended him as a great athlete.

"I'm serious, sir," the young man replied. "I'm a kicker."

"What college did you go to?" asked the assistant coach.

"University of Afghanistan," replied the man.

"You're a veteran?"

"Yes, sir. I'm a Marine."

"Thank you for your service, but we have kickers. I don't think we need another one."

"I've encountered many obstacles, sir. I should have died many times, but each time God saved me. I prayed for guidance as to what to do, and it came to me in a dream that I should be a kicker."

The assistant coach was a tall African American man named Eugene Eckley. He had been a linebacker on several professional teams and had retired as a player a dozen years ago. His brother had been killed in Afghanistan. He knew this boy had no chance at making the team, but something inside him wanted to try to help him.

"Son, there are many job programs for veterans. Have you ever kicked for a school team before?"

"I played in high school, but after my father died I enlisted in the Marines."

"Don't you have any other family?"

"I want to make this my new family, sir."

"Son, this is pro football. Few athletes can compete at this level, and to try to do it without any college training, you'd have no chance."

"Sir, if the war taught me anything, it was that if I'm willing to take chances, I'll have chances."

The assistant coach looked down toward the ground. This kid had no chance, but he was a nice young man and a Marine. He deserved at least a shot. The thought ran through his mind that this could have been his brother.

"What's your name, son?"

"John Thaddeus. My name is John, sir."

"Where did you come from?"

"I walked from Paterson. I read in the newspaper this is where your training camp is."

"How did you walk all of this way?"

"I'm a Marine, sir," John said as a smile broke out on his face.

The assistant coach thought for a minute. He'd seen a lot of athletes who had done a lot of things to try out for the team, but none had done what this man had done. He obviously had heart. The assistant coach looked into John's eyes, and John looked back. It was as if he could see into John's soul. It was clear and good. Something moved him to act.

"Come with me, John. I'm not making any promises."

While all of this was occurring on the sidelines, the other athletes were doing calisthenics on the field. Eugene walked young John over to the head coach, Jeff Schindler. "Coach, I've got a walk-on here as a placekicker."

"We already have kickers. You know that." The coach seemed mildly annoyed at this distraction.

"I know," said Eugene, "but this kid is a Marine and walked here from Paterson to try out. I thought maybe we could give him a chance. He may catch on with another team if he's any good. Anyway, he's a Marine." The head coach knew about Eugene's brother.

"A Marine, huh? What's your name, son?"

"My name is John, sir."

"You walked from Paterson?"

"Yes, sir."

"Where did you play college ball?"

"In Afghanistan, sir."

"You're kidding? You never played in college?"

"No, sir."

"What makes you think you can play pro ball?"

"No one told me I couldn't, sir."

"You must be crazy, son, but since you're a Marine and you walked this far, hang around and I'll drive you home after practice."

"I have no place to stay, sir."

"What? Where do you plan to go?"

"I expect to make the team and play pro ball, sir."

"Where have you been staying?"

"A friend of mine, Sister Francis, got one of my old teachers to let me stay in his basement for a few days."

"I must be crazy," said the coach as he looked at Eugene, "but stay here, and after practice I'll let you kick a few balls."

"Thank you, sir."

Practice continued and eventually ended. True to his word, the coach called to John, who had been standing on the sidelines.

"Okay, warm up, and I'll let you kick a few balls to show us what you've got."

Eugene had now wandered back over to watch. "Should I get the special teams coach to watch?"

"Yeah, go ahead, but make it quick. It's late."

The special teams coach, Frank Purcell, joined the group. After being introduced and having the situation explained to him, he asked the ball boys to set up a ball on the tee at the forty-yard line of the kicking team.

"I want to see if you can even reach the end zone. John, do you want to change your clothes?"

"No need. I'm ready."

"Okay, kid," Frank said. "Go kick a few."

"Yes, sir," said John. He ran onto the field in his Nike sneakers, leaving his knapsack and jacket on the sidelines.

John lined up. He did not kick as most NFL kickers did—in a soccer style setup—but addressed the ball straight on as the old-style kickers did. As he kicked, the ball launched off the tee as if shot from a cannon. It traveled fast and high, and the coaches watched as it passed yard marker after yard marker on its way toward the end zone. But then something happened. The ball did not drop into the end zone, as many kickoff balls did, nor did it go through the end zone on a bounce. The ball passed easily through the uprights of the goalpost before it fell to the ground.

John smiled easily and turned toward the coaches. The coaches' mouths dropped open. They had never seen this before. They had many years of coaching among them, but this was new. They looked at the ball and each other and then back to John. *Who was this kid?*

"Kick another one, son," said Frank.

John did so. He kicked five more balls, and four out of five followed the same trajectory, while the fifth missed the goalposts to the left by only inches. The coaches looked at each other and started laughing.

"John, come over here. Where did you learn to kick like that?" asked the kicking team coach.

"My father taught me before he passed away."

"How about your mom?" asked the head coach.

"She's gone too, sir."

"Where are you staying?"

"As I told you, I have been staying in a room in Paterson that a nun I know got for me. She was my high school principal and helped take care of my mother when she got sick. And she wrote to me when I was in the service."

The head coach spoke up. "No, you go with Eugene. Eugene, get John a room in the dorms with the other players. We'll get you set up for tonight, and tomorrow we'll give you a real workout and see what you can do."

John smiled but didn't seem surprised. "Thank you, sir. I look forward to it."

The training camp was being held at a local university, where the players were staying in dorms and eating in the cafeteria.

John was shown to a room he would share with an African American rookie who was a wide receiver.

"Hi, I'm Wade Jenkins," this young man stated forcefully while extending his hand in firm friendship toward John.

"Wade, this is John Thaddeus. He'll be your roommate for a few days. John, say hello to Wade," said Eugene.

"Hello," said John. "What position do you play?"

"I'm a wide receiver, I hope," said Wade with a laugh. "What about you?"

"I'm a placekicker. I'm just a walk-on, but I'll try my best. I don't know, but I think I can do this," John said, looking down now and a little pensive.

"Where did you go to school?" asked Wade.

"I'm recently discharged from the Marines," said John. "I went to Our Lady of Lourdes High School in Paterson."

"Did you go to college?" asked Wade.

"No. My father died, and I kind of lost my way, so my mom and my high school principal, Sister Francis, suggested I join the Marines,"

John said with a reflective look on his face. Wade could see there was a lot behind the story, but he did not feel he knew John well enough to ask for more. There would be time to find out later.

"Wade, is there a pay phone close by? I need to call Sister Francis. She will be worried about me."

"I haven't seen a pay phone around here, but you can use my cell," said Wade.

"Are you sure you don't mind?" asked John.

"Yes. I have unlimited minutes. Go ahead."

"Thanks, man. I'll be back in a minute." John walked down the hall to a spot near a window that was relatively quiet. He dialed the number. An elderly female voice answered.

"Hello? This is Sister Francis."

"Sister, it's John. I tried out for an NFL team as a kicker. It's not settled, but they asked me to stay for a tryout."

"Where are you?" Sister asked.

"I'm at the training camp in Madison. I'm okay. I'm really excited about the opportunity. Please say a prayer for me."

"I'm glad you called. I was getting worried about you," said Sister. "I'll say a rosary for you. You can be anything you want to be, John!"

"Thanks. Don't worry, Sister. I'm okay."

"When is the tryout? I want to come."

"Sister, you can't come to an NFL tryout!"

"Why not? I used to run track and play football as a girl. You are not going to try out for this team unless I think they're a good group!"

John was laughing now. After all, he was a Marine and was fresh from a tour of duty in Afghanistan, yet Sister Frances had not changed; John knew better than to try to change her mind.

"John, where is the practice facility?"

"It's on a college campus in north Jersey."

"What time?"

"I don't know, Sister. I appreciate the thought, but you don't have to come."

"Nonsense! I'll be there at eight tomorrow morning." With that, Sister hung up the phone. John smiled. He loved that old nun, and he knew she loved him. She had paid his tuition for his last year of parochial high school when his mother could not afford it. Having helped him spiritually, she now felt responsible for him, especially since his mother had passed.

A good high school principal gets to know the students in her care. John's story was a sad one. John's father had been an alcoholic. He'd been a carpenter by trade but was a mediocre craftsman, and when he had difficulty getting work he would turn to alcohol. To make matters worse, in the seventh grade John broke his right leg while running in a park. It took a long time to heal, and the muscles in his right leg seemed to atrophy while in the cast. John desperately wanted to play football, but the doctors told him that would not be possible. His leg was too badly damaged, and he could not risk being tackled.

Sister Francis walked down the hall in school one afternoon and heard sobbing coming from the boys' locker room. The other boys had suited up for football practice, but John couldn't play because of his leg. Sister

9

poked her head into the locker room and saw John, then a freshman, all alone. She entered and sat down next to him.

"Now, now; what's wrong?" she asked.

"I want to play football, but with this leg I can't play," John sobbed in response.

"Aren't you John Thaddeus?"

"Yes, Sister. I broke my leg in a fall, and I can't play."

"My son, this leg can be a blessing or a curse. It will be a curse if you let it ruin you and a blessing if you learn a very valuable lesson that you must overcome the obstacles in your path and that with God all things are possible. Stop crying now! You go home and come back to see me after school tomorrow."

"Okay, Sister." John stopped sobbing and stood, grabbed his book bag, and walked out of the room, wiping his eyes to hide the tears.

There was no way Sister Francis was going to let something as trivial as a broken leg hold back one of her students. That night she went to the chapel in the convent where she lived and prayed the rosary for John and for guidance. She knew God would open another door, but she also knew about John's family troubles. Little escaped the purview of this old nun. She was extremely dedicated. These were her students, and she believed she was responsible for them and considered it her sacred responsibility to bring them to God. She thought helping John overcome this problem would give him hope and teach him how to overcome other obstacles he might encounter on his path to becoming a good man. So she prayed, and it came to her. Sister had run track in her youth while at high school, and she had developed strong legs as a result. So the next morning she cornered the track coach and, after explaining the situation, persuaded him to let John come out for cross-country track. This way he'd avoid the physical beating of football but gain confidence and strength. The track coach sensed a development project and tried to talk his way out of it, but once an idea took hold in Sister Francis's mind no one could dislodge it.

So, John went out for track. He was not the fastest runner, but he had good stamina. He would run at least ten miles after school each day, rain or shine, with the exception of snow. He was then being trained not only by the coach but also by Sister Francis, who asked no quarter and gave none when it came to doing what was necessary to develop her students.

During that track season, John still missed football, so his father suggested he would teach John how to kick. That would involve less contact than any other position on the team. John's father had been on a semi-pro soccer team in his youth. He showed John exercises to strengthen his leg and taught him to keep his head in the game no matter what the circumstance. John would run in the afternoons and kick when he got home and on weekends. John and his father practiced for hours. John had a tremendous appetite, so he did not develop the frail appearance of a runner. His legs became extremely strong, and his junior year he tried out to be a kicker and made the football team.

Football was great, but Sister made John continue to run and to drink a protein concoction she had read about in a magazine to strengthen his muscles. John did not have full lateral mobility in his right leg, so he could not kick in the style of soccer kickers. This is why he learned to kick straight on. All of that running, those special shakes, his practice, his natural athletic ability, the prayers of Sister Francis, and her constant application of Lourdes water to John's right leg helped to strengthen his leg.

In addition, there was another factor. One day, while walking home from the store, John's father saw that someone had put out a StairMaster for the bulk trash pickup. A thought ran through his head. He called a friend, and together they came the night before the scheduled bulk

11

pickup and took the StairMaster home. Every night after John practiced kicking, John's father would watch his son work on the StairMaster. The machine was designed to mimic walking up stairs, and John's father thought it would strengthen John's legs. For years John would work on the StairMaster at night. After his father's death, he worked even harder, because it had been something they had done together. Over time the weakest part of John's body grew to become the strongest, so that when he tried out to be a kicker on the high school team, his leg was unbelievably strong. He could kick a mile. He consistently made sixty-yard field goals and even once made a sixty-nine yarder.

Sister had invested much in John and also got to know his mother, who would come to school for parent-teacher conferences. Her name was Joan, and she was Irish Catholic. She had learned to suffer patiently in resignation because of the drunkenness of her husband and his inability to produce enough income for the family. She had taken a job as an orderly at the local hospital to help make ends meet.

Suddenly, at the beginning of John's senior year, his father died from a heart attack, and John and his mother were left alone. There was now no money for the private Catholic high school John was attending, but when John went to withdraw and transfer to the public school, Sister Francis would have none of it. Sister did not make much money, but she paid the tuition herself. She gave much because she felt she had been given much.

Sister had contracted leukemia when she was a young novitiate in her order, the Daughters of Mary Help of Christians, a companion order to the Salesians, which is a teaching order founded by the great Don Bosco to help young boys. The Daughters of Mary Help of Christians had been founded by St. Mary Mazzarello to help young girls. After the diagnosis, Sister made a pilgrimage to Lourdes, France, to pray to Our Lady of Lourdes to allow her to complete her vocation and help youngsters. On her flight home from the trip, she had such a feeling of peace. It was as if the hand of God had been placed on her head and the power of God had gone through her whole body.

When she returned, Sister went through painful spinal taps and much treatment, but her faith never failed. She anointed herself each day with the blessed Lourdes water given by the great Mother of God for healing at the spring in Lourdes, France.

In the end, Sister's leukemia went into remission. Now, many years later, Sister thanked God that He had given her more time to serve Him. She was on a mission. There was no way she was not going to help John. She was, as it were, another guardian angel sent by God to help children. This was her life.

But it was not to be a smooth ride for John. In his senior year, John began to get into fights at school with other players. His father's death and the family's financial problems angered him, and his mother's long hours working additional shifts to make money did not allow sufficient time for her to help quell his anger. His mother felt he needed more discipline. So in the spring of his senior year, his mother, in consultation with Sister Francis, decided to take him down to the Marine recruiting station, and John enlisted.

The Marine training gave John discipline and purpose. It taught him to channel his anger into focusing on his mission and the men around him. His strong legs allowed him to walk and run great distances. He was not fast, but he was very strong. In time he was assigned to the Force Recon platoon and was sent to Afghanistan. He went on long patrols and saw many men killed or wounded; this deepened his spirituality and his confidence. Since he had not been killed, despite all he had been through, his fear dissipated, and his self-confidence and faith increased. Just as the StairMaster had strengthened his legs, so the exercise of his courage, concern for his mission and comrades, and his experience in Afghanistan had strengthened his character and his faith and trust God. While his time in the Marines was not without troubles and sorrow, he gave thanks for his blessings.

John never forgot Sister Francis's kindness. When he went into the Marines, Sister had given him a scapular and a Lourdes rosary that she had brought back from her trip to Lourdes, France. She told him to wear the scapular always so that the great Mother of God would watch over him. She also told him to pray the rosary when times got tough and he needed help or healing. She wished him goodbye, wrote him often, and sent him cookies at Christmas and on his birthday. Although great distances separated them, Sister became his guiding force, like a good parent. She became his second guardian angel, and he loved her dearly. As he grew to be a man in the fields of Afghanistan, he thought of her often, and his respect and love for her deepened. This deepened even more after his mother died of breast cancer while John was deployed. On occasion, John would experience fear and anxiety in response to the things he saw in Afghanistan, and he vented about these things in his letters to Sister Francis. He had always shared his fears with her, and encountering people's fear of death was not new to her. She wrote back and comforted John "You shall not fear the terror of the night nor the arrow that flies by day … Though a thousand fall at your side, ten thousand at your right hand, near you it shall not come… For he commands his angels with regard to you, to guard you wherever you go (Psalm 91: 5,7,11 NABRE).

While the Marines gave him patience, focus, strength, and courage, it was Sister Francis who gave him faith and love and the will to carry on despite his fears. Gradually, the hole in his soul from his father's death closed. All his experiences had taught him to overcome, to adapt, and to be independent. He was his own man, but more importantly, as a gift from God, he was a man of faith. The rosary Sister had given him had been his lifeline in combat. He would grasp it as if his very life depended on it. It had become part of his soul.

When John was discharged, Sister Francis insisted he come to see her right away. She got him a room in the personal home of one of the lay teachers whose wife had passed away and whose children had long since left home. John's mother's death had been slow and painful, but Sister Francis helped get her into a nursing home run by the Little Sisters of the Poor, where angels nursed her until her death. John was immensely grateful to Sister Francis, so he did whatever she asked.

Coming out of his experiences in the Marines, and with Sister Francis as an additional angel on his shoulder, John began to think about the focus and purpose of his life. What did he want to work and live for? He had learned that what others thought did not matter. It would not be enough to acquire wealth. He knew that money would only be a test of whether he was a true servant. He realized he needed to go to college. However, before that, there was something he wanted to try. So when he read in the newspaper that an NFL training camp was starting in New Jersey, he was inspired to try out as a kicker. He loved football, and he had seen so much loss in Afghanistan that he needed more than an academic focus at the moment. He prayed, and the inspiration seemed to urge him on. It was crazy, but he was a Marine; overcoming obstacles is what Marines do. He would give it his total commitment. John did not focus on the risks or the negatives. He controlled his thoughts; his focus was on what was possible and the mental attitude he would need to achieve it.

He had overcome more than this. He had been tested by adversity and learned much from his suffering. He learned to trust in and rely on God completely. He also learned that although some of the events that caused him to suffer were evil, God intended them for good. He would not go through life focusing on his hardships; rather, he would look outward to help others.

But he loved football, and his prayers did not seem to point him in a different direction. He would step aside to give it a shot. He figured he could serve wherever he went. But, having seen so much death, he thought often of his own death, of what he wanted to be, how he would be evaluated on his deathbed, and what he wanted to accomplish before then. However, surely this temporary dalliance would fit into God's plan for his life. For his part, he would keep God's presence ever in his mind. He would make everything he did an unspoken prayer. Surely that would be enough for then. If he were successful, he would give all the glory to God and would not attribute the success to any talents or efforts of his own. These were his thoughts as he contemplated trying out for the team.

The next day was a beautiful sunny day. John arose around six. Breakfast was at seven, and practice started at eight. John made his way to the practice field, where Sister Francis was waiting for him. Rather than a habit, she wore a simple, inexpensive, but smart blue suit and a pin reflecting her religious order. John had had no doubt she would be there. She greeted John with a hug and wished him well. Other players looked on quizzically. *Who was this woman? Could she be this rookie's mother? Are you kidding?* No one had ever seen such a thing at a closed practice.

Eugene came over to John. "John, practice is closed. Who is that?"

"That's Sister Francis, my high school principal. I told her not to come, but you don't know Sister Francis," John said with a smile. "If you want her to leave, you go tell her!"

One glance told Eugene all he needed to know. Sister had taken residence where she was and had pulled out her rosary beads. She was praying, but her eyes didn't miss a single event on the field in front of her.

The coach then came over and also inquired. John just looked down and smiled. He gave the same explanation. The coach was not about to start a fight with an old nun. So practice went on, and all tried to ignore her, but all noticed her and wondered.

Practice at this early stage of training camp started off with drills and calisthenics. They didn't need to wear pads yet, but the two-a-day practices were designed to decide on the best talent for the team. There were 110 players in camp, but the number would have to be winnowed down for the final team. John participated in calisthenics, but many of the drills were designed for the lineman, wideouts, running backs, and quarterbacks. The kickers were a little different: three other placekickers were trying out for the team, as well as four punters. The placekickers gathered together on one side of the field, warming up and practicing their kicking motions. There was Michael Connell, the previous year's kicker. He was good but had missed a few key field goals longer than forty yards. He was accurate within forty yards, but, as he aged, his leg was not as strong as some others for longer kicks.

Another kicker was from Clemson, a journeyman who lacked flash. He was good and reliable but was an eighth-round draft pick when nothing more attractive was on the board. The other kicker was a walk-on from Rutgers but had little chance of unseating the incumbent from last year. And then there was John. Who was this guy? Where had he played? They asked him, and he told them. They all wrote him off as a nice guy who had no chance, but they forgot he was a Marine. He was trained to overcome, to stand up to pressure, to exceed expectations, and to accomplish his mission. That's what Marines do. Besides, Sister Francis had been tougher than any drill instructor and had taught him that nothing was impossible with God. John believed it down to his soul. He was a Marine who had faith, and that would be an unbeatable combination.

John couldn't wait to get started. The kicking coach asked the men to line up and take turns kicking off. The other three kickers performed pretty much as expected. The first kick was a thirty-yard field goal. Last year's player, Michael Connell, made the kick. The kid from Clemson did as well, but the walk-on from Rutgers was wide left. John's kick was true. At forty-five yards, the Clemson kid made it, and Mike did as well but only barely. John's kick was through with plenty of leg.

At fifty yards, all missed except John. Mike was short—just not enough leg. The kid from Clemson was long enough but pushed the ball right. The kid from Rutgers was short and wide left. Finally came fifty-five yards. Only John made it, seemingly with plenty of leg left.

"Okay, kid," said the coach as John made the fifty-five-yarder. "Do you think you could do sixty yards, Marine?"

"Hoorah!" shouted John. Nothing more was needed. He made sixty and sixty-five but missed to the left at seventy and was barely long enough. Still, he had impressed. The coach was giddy. John was satisfied with his performance. Sister Francis just continued praying. She showed no emotion but took everything in. She was praying for something bigger for John. John looked over at her, and he knew it. He could read her mind. He had always been able to do so. She was entirely predictable. She was a total joy, and in her he could see all the virtues. He really loved that old nun.

Coach dismissed the young men from practice to go to lunch. All the kickers congratulated John and wanted to interrogate him about his background and training over lunch. He was the only one who did not kick soccer style. John was polite but quickly took his leave to jog over to see Sister Francis.

"Sister, what did you think?"

"Thank God, John; he gave your legs the strength."

"I remember your help, Sister. You came and prayed over me and put Lourdes water on my legs. You helped me, and you gave me the will to carry on. Thank you."

"Nonsense. God gave you those things. Give thanks to Him."

"How about lunch, Sister?"

"Okay. Where can we go?" Sister asked, looking around.

"I think we can eat in the cafeteria. Let's walk there." On the way, Sister reflected out loud. She was always self-reflective, but this time she gave voice to her thoughts in front of John. It was his pleasure to overhear the thoughts of an angel.

"I was in New York City the other day. It's so busy there, millions of souls. I began to reflect. There are over six billion people in the world today. And we know from tradition that each soul is so precious that God assigns a guardian angel to watch over and to safeguard it. Now, if there are over six billion people in the world, I guess that means there are at least six billion angels to watch over them. Add up the number of people since the foundation of the world, and just think of the number of saints and angels in heaven. Think then of the size of the heavenly kingdom, and add to that what I heard the other day. Scientists saw the light of a star a hundred billion light-years away. Just imagine it: a hundred billion light-years away. The universe is unbelievably old and immense, and God, who runs it all, also created all of it. How insignificant we are, and yet He sent His only son to save us. Even after we crucified Him, He still forgave us. Even with all that vastness in the universe, His son has told us that sooner would heaven and earth pass away than His word pass away, and with His word He has told us of His great mercy to a contrite soul. Now, if God has promised to clothe the universe in such mercy, how much will He do for you? There is no need ever to be weak in faith."

The message was not lost on John. He been happy about practice, but he was anxious that he might be inadequate to the task since he had never played college ball. Sister knew what he needed before he even asked. She had the gift of perception and could tell a soul's longing, even before it was expressed in words.

"Thank you, Sister. I needed that," John said with a smile as he gazed into Sister's heavily wrinkled face, which looked as if the weight of the world and all its troubled souls had taken their toll on it. John knew she was truly special.

They had a nice lunch. The coaches had asked John to have lunch at the practice facility and had invited Sister as well. How could they not invite an old nun to have lunch? Sister had a small salad. John made a turkey sandwich on rye bread and finished off lunch with a banana. They sat at the far end of the cafeteria. All the players noticed. The other kickers were jealous of John's performance. The big defensive end, Harvey Brown, was irritated. He resented the nun's presence at lunch. He was used to holding court, bullying his fellow teammates, loudly telling jokes, and mouthing profanities. This was their luncheon and their team, with no room for outsiders. Furthermore, this was a man's team, fully macho. There was room for mothers, whether actual or supposed. He resented any tilt toward softness or compassion. He fashioned himself as a man's man and the leader of the pack. The presence of this nun cramped his style. Further, this kicker was only a walk-on, not a veteran; nor was he a number one draft choice as Harvey had been. He had been All-Pro four times in his six years on the team. The team didn't need a mother; he was the father, or at least a big brother, and that was enough. He would hold his tongue for then while the nun was there. But he was not a religious man. He was too self-absorbed and refused to acknowledge he needed anybody or anything. In his mind, he set the tone and the culture around him. He was a fighter and, like many men of his size, only respected strength, because that's what he had. He would deal with this weak-kneed newcomer on the practice field.

Sister and John finished their lunch, and John walked Sister to her car before rejoining the team on the practice field. Sister drove an old white compact Ford. As John walked onto the field, Harvey rushed him and dipped his left shoulder to hit John's right flank. It was a glancing blow but a clear signal of disrespect and dominance. Harvey ran past John onto the field without an apology. John was not seriously injured, but he felt the blow and got the message. John looked up to see Harvey running to the center of the field where the linemen were gathered. Some of them had noticed the affront but said nothing. You didn't cross Harvey, a team captain. Besides, this was pre-season, and everyone was fighting for a place on the team. There were no friends here, only competitors. They would not become friends until the team was formed and all the cuts had been made. John said nothing. He absorbed the blow. He sensed not to say anything. In any event, he was a Marine, and Marines don't whine.

Practice continued with the players put through drills under the watchful eyes of the coaches. John continued to impress by making every field goal and sending kickoffs through the end zone, precluding any ability for a speedy receiver to return the kick the length of the field. Two of the other kickers were good but could not match John's strength and accuracy. The coaches could see it, and the other kickers knew it too. Harvey continued to keep an eye on John and peppered John with nasty comments and jokes both on the field and in the locker room. No one came to John's aid. All joined in Harvey's amusement at belittling John.

"Where did you go to college, army boy?" asked Harvey

"I'm a Marine, not army." John said matter-of-factly.

"Well, excuse the heck out of me," said Harvey. "Well, where did you go?"

John did not answer. But in not answering, everyone knew the answer. Harvey had found a weakness he could exploit. "Where did you go, navy boy?" Again, John did not answer. Harvey walked over with a threatening look on his face. "I'm talking to you, boy."

"You talk too much and say too little," said John. Surrender was not in his creed. John did not know how to back down. Harvey, having been challenged in front of the whole team, acted livid whether he actually was or not. He moved menacingly toward John. He weighed 260, and John only weighed 190. John was no match physically, but he turned to

21

face Harvey. Before the confrontation could take place other teammates stepped between them. John was the best kicker. No one thought it would be good if the two fought. John dressed quickly and left.

Two-a-day practices continued, as did Harvey's harassment. John remained oblivious. He cared not for the thoughts of men. He was uninterested in anything that was not of God. John focused on his mission, not on the surrounding distractions. The Marines and Sister Francis had taught him that.

There was just something about John that angered Harvey. Maybe it was the fact that he had not gone to college, while all the other players had been schooled in top college programs around the country. In Harvey's mind this made John an amateur. He was undrafted, a walk-on. Who was this guy? In addition, he was a Marine, a tough guy. In Harvey's mind, Harvey was the toughest guy, and everyone needed to know that. Maybe it was John's independence. Harvey didn't seem to be able to get to him, and that meant Harvey couldn't control and subjugate him the way he had been able to subjugate others. Maybe it was because John was the new hotshot in camp. Anyway, Harvey just didn't like him.

John would go to his room at night and only leave briefly for dinner, unless there was a team meeting. He did not focus on the frills. As a Marine, he was used to Spartan conditions, and he was okay with that.

2

THE CHANCE

Training camp was winding down, and final cuts were being made. John had gone through camp with the best record of any of the kickers. He had made 90 percent of his field goals, and he could make the longest field goals of any of the kickers. He had impressed the coaches, but there was that nagging question. He was not the product of a college program. There was not a long track record of his accomplishments as a kicker. How would he hold up under pressure with the game on the line? The other kickers were more of a known commodity. They wouldn't choke. Maybe their legs weren't as strong, but there had been a four-year track record to look back on in college and, in the case of one of the kickers, his time as a member of an NFL team–*this* team. Lastly, the coaches had become aware of Harvey's criticisms, and while they knew Harvey and were not overly concerned by his comments, there was the potential for team discord and morale problems if John missed an important field goal when some key members of the team already didn't like him. On balance, the coaches thought the safe choice was to go with the previous year's kicker, and John was cut from the team in the final cut.

John was disappointed, but he had overcome worse. He took a job at the local grocery store. It was a tough job, but it was money, the people were pleasant, and it put food on the table. He rented the room he had been staying in before he had moved into the dorms during tryouts. He worked as many hours as he could. While he considered it to be only a temporary job, he enjoyed the serenity of it. It was a chance to decompress and quiet his mind from the hypervigilance of combat. He would apply to colleges the next year.

The football season began, and the team was doing well—until fate took a hand. Just before the third game of the season, the team's placekicker was jogging, tripped, and badly sprained his ankle, which made kicking long field goals no longer possible. The other kickers were no match for John's talent, so the decision was made: John got the call to come back for a tryout. John came back. He knew God would open another door, but this one was a surprise. His tryout impressed the coaches again, and he was signed to finish the season. John was elated and called Sister Francis to share his joy and ask her to attend his first game. Sister loved both John and football, so she gleefully accepted.

THE FIRST GAME

The first game John played in was against Miami. The Raptors were favored to win, and it was pretty much a lopsided game. John's kickoffs went through the end zone on each occasion, so no run back by Miami was possible. He made three extra points and two field goals, but they were relatively short: forty-one yards and thirty-five yards. The game was a victory, and John made no mistakes. The coaches and John's teammates were happy with John—except for Harvey. Harvey had only contempt for John, which was his way of trying to gain dominance. John would only smile at him and refuse to engage in any confrontation.

Practices went well for the next game against Dallas, but Dallas would be a tougher challenge. John kicked well in practice, and knowing it would be a tougher game, he concentrated on practicing longer field goals in the fifty-yard range. This didn't escape the coaches' view. They knew that the kicking game could be more important because Dallas had a better defense, especially in the red zone, and scoring touchdowns could be a lot harder. Privately, they remained concerned about how this untried and unproven kicker would stand up to Dallas's more intense rush during field goal attempts as well as to the general pressure of the game. But it was too late to change. They would have to trust John and hope for the best.

The game started fast. Dallas won the toss, marched down the field, and scored a touchdown. Their running game was working, and that opened up the passing game, including a thirty-four-yard completion on a big pass play down the Raptors' side of the field.

The Raptors received the ball and ran it back to their own twenty-yard line but went three and out. They couldn't get their running game going and on two consecutive runs were stopped for no gain and a three-yard gain, respectively. On third down, they completed a short pass on the right side of the field, but the receiver was tackled short of a first down.

The Raptors' punter kicked, and Dallas received on its own thirty-yard line, where the receiver was tackled for no gain. Dallas's first pass was a long bomb, but it was overthrown. Their next pass went for twelve yards, and the receiver was immediately tackled, but it was good enough for a first down. Their running back continued to rip off chunks of yardage of between seven and ten yards, which set up a touchdown pass to Dallas's tight end down the middle. The score was now fourteen to zero, in favor of Dallas.

The offensive coordinator for the Raptors realized the Raptors needed to score. If they fell behind by three touchdowns, it would be hard to come back against Dallas's defense. It was time to open up the offense. Instead of trying to establish the run, they would try to establish a short passing game and use the run to keep the defense honest. The hope was that over time, as the safeties for the defense came to expect short passes and cheated up to stop the completions, some big plays down the field to the tight end could open up. The Raptors began with this strategy. They successfully completed a number of short passes to their wide receivers but initially avoided passes to the tight end until he could open up on a deeper route down the middle. They ran a few running plays that didn't gain much but served to keep the defense honest. They moved the ball down the field, but the defense stiffened in the red zone, and they were unable to score a touchdown. It was then John's job to kick a forty-yard field goal. The snap was good, and the rush was ferocious, but the offensive line picked it up; John made the kick with no problem. The score was then fourteen to three.

Dallas lined up to receive the kickoff, but John's kick went through the end zone; the ball was placed on the twenty-yard line with no run back. The Raptors then placed six men in the box and were able to stop any more decent runs by Dallas. With the Dallas running game unable to achieve first downs, Dallas tried to stretch the field with a few long pass plays, but the Raptors' cornerbacks provided good coverage. On a forty-yard pass attempt, the pass fell short of the receiver, so the Raptor safety was able to pick it off and run it back to Dallas's forty-yard line. However, the Raptors were unable to move the ball, so it fell to the coaches to choose whether to try a fifty-yard field goal or to punt and try to hit the coffin corner in order to pin Dallas back within the ten-yard line. The head coach was about to send in the punter, but before he could act John ran out onto the field; seeing John run out, his kick holder also ran out. The coach was furious, but he didn't want to waste a time-out this early to stop it; plus, he was beginning to develop some confidence in John, so he choked down his anger and crossed his fingers. The ball was hiked a little high, but the holder was the backup quarterback and was used to handling the ball; he quickly spun it so the laces faced the goalposts just in time for John to make the kick. A moment of panic went through the coach's mind, but before real fear could set in, John made the kick—a little off to the left side but clearly through the goalposts. John didn't even wait for the ball to go through. He kicked the ball and immediately turned to run off the field. He showed no celebration, no doubt, and barely a smile. It was as if it was so common for him to make the kick that the times for celebration had long since passed. John exuded a quiet confidence, but he was still an unproven commodity. The score was now fourteen to six.

The ball changed hands back and forth for the rest of the half, but neither team was able to score. The Raptors intercepted Dallas once more but couldn't score and couldn't even get close enough for a fifty-yard field goal. The coach was not prepared to let John try a field goal of longer than fifty yards so early in the game because of the field position it would give Dallas if he missed. He had yelled at John on the sidelines for running out onto the field, so John knew not to do that again.

After the half, the Raptors received the ball and John made two more field goals, but Dallas also made one field goal; the score stood at seventeen to twelve. The game ebbed and flowed, but finally with a minute and a half left, the Raptors scored a touchdown, bringing the score to nineteen to seventeen. The Raptors won the game.

4

THE IN-BETWEENS

Not everything in football is the game. There are also the in-betweens. There are days off, practices, get-togethers with teammates, friendships and adversaries made and lost, competition between players for playing time, relationships with the coaches, and every day life. All of these things are important because football is a team sport, and to be a successful team, all the parts must work together in harmony. It is very hard for a team in disharmony to pull together and achieve success. No one can do it alone, and the players must feel that the other members of the team have their backs. But there was a problem this year.

The kicker is always kind of off to the side, alone. The kicker doesn't enjoy the natural camaraderie of the offensive line or defensive line or the linebackers or the defensive backs or the running backs. But John was even more alone because of his rivalry with Harvey. There was a tension between them that all could feel. Harvey was used to dominating and conquering both on and off the field. That was who he was. John, on the other hand, did not bow to any man. If Harvey failed to subjugate John, his domination of others would also be in jeopardy. He knew no other way. As one of the leaders of the team, Harvey knew others on the team would follow his lead. How often the crowd will follow the leader, whether or not it makes sense! So much is this a truth that there is even a children's game called "follow the leader." But the crowd can be fickle, which Harvey sensed: he did not want anything to interfere with his domination. It was important to him not to lose the crowd.

All of this made John even more of an outsider, yet he did not seem to care. He was a Marine. He would survive and overcome as he had learned to do. He also had God to rely on. He had learned that from Sister Francis. John's independence and faith were evident to anyone who saw him. That was who he was. He respected authority but only legitimate authority.

The punter on a football team also stands alone in a certain sense. Accordingly, the punter often feels some kinship to the placekicker. How often it is that like attracts like, and people facing similar problems can be drawn to one another.

"Hi, John. My name is Phil Ryan. I'm the punter."

"Hello," said John with a smile. The two shook hands.

"We kickers have to stick together," said Phil.

"I understand," responded John, still smiling.

So the friendship began. Phil brought John coffee the next morning, and John was pleased. It was an offering of friendship, and John was open to it. As a Marine, he knew how to build relationships with others on the team.

"Thanks, Phil. Just the way I like it, light and sweet, although I also got used to black coffee in the service. What are you doing for lunch?"

"Nothing," said Phil.

"Good, let's go together. I'll find you at lunchtime."

"Great," said Phil. "See you then."

The team provided lunch for the players on days when they practiced and meals when they played. The two walked to lunch together. They sat at a separate table together. Many players noticed but didn't pay much attention. No one much cared what the kickers did, except for Harvey. He looked over and scowled, but he was busy holding court with the defensive line. The same pattern continued day after day.

Phil had been a kicker in the league for nine years. He and his wife had married in his first year of college after she got pregnant, and they had a son who was now thirteen. They loved each other and had carved out a life together. But there seemed to be sadness in Phil. John thought he had sensed it, but he didn't know Phil well enough to be certain. Over time, the signs became more obvious, and Phil began to develop dark circles under his eyes and seemed distracted.

One day after practice the two were walking toward the parking lot where, by chance, their cars were parked close together. They stood for a moment and made conversation.

"Phil, stop me if it's none of my business, but you seem distracted. Is there anything I can help with? We are friends, so I hope you'll think of me if you need help."

Phil looked down. A tear rolled down his cheek. "It's my son. He's hanging around with the wrong crowd, and I found drugs in his room. I confronted him, but he just stormed out of the room and yelled at me, saying he won't give up his friends. I don't know what to do. I don't know what to do. I don't know what to do." Phil's voice got a little lower each time he repeated this, and he shook his head left and right as he spoke. The progressive weakness in his voice seemed to match the progressive weakness he felt in dealing with this problem.

"Phil," John said as he grabbed Phil's arms with both hands. "I'm going to help you. I know just what to do. I've got the solution."

"What's that?" Phil asked hopefully.

"Sister Francis," John said with a smile on his face.

"Sister Francis?" asked Phil.

"Sister Francis," said John. "Not to worry. I'll reach out to her. Believe me. You've never met anyone like her. I think she trained the drill sergeants in the Marines. She'll whip your son into shape."

John called Sister Francis. She arrived at practice the next day at seven o'clock in the morning, the time she had agreed on with John. Phil was there as well and told the story to Sister Francis.

"Okay," said Sister. "Here's what we're going to do. What's your son's name?"

"Phil Junior."

"Bring Phil Junior to Our Lady of Lourdes Catholic High School in Paterson tomorrow at eight o'clock in the morning."

"He won't go. I told you about our fight over his friends."

"Who's the parent, you or him?" asked Sister Francis. She had come a long, hard way. She had seen many problems. She was loving but tough. No child's tantrum was going to stand in her way. She would straighten his behind out quick.

What happened? Not without some pain and tears, Phil Junior was brought as requested. Sister Francis had not failed anyone before, and she had no intention of failing this boy and his family. She was over them like white on rice. Phil Junior was transferred to Our Lady of Lourdes High School. Sister Francis met the boy every morning when his father dropped him off, checked on him at lunch, and had the football coach sign him up for football, with a word from Sister Francis about the problem. Phil Junior didn't have time to breathe. At her direction, his father took away his cell phone and had the house line disconnected. He was not allowed out at night and was given three hours of homework every day after practice, which didn't end until six o'clock in the evening, when his father or mother picked him up.

Phil Junior didn't know what hit him. If he thought he could outsmart an old nun, he was sadly mistaken. She had dealt with many problems in her time as a nun. This was just one more. She prayed for Phil Junior and the family each day and in her nightly rosary. She put the problem in God's hands, and since she was His instrument, she had no intention of failing. Phil Junior was beginning to straighten out, and Phil, the football player, would be forever grateful to Sister Francis and to John, but most of all to God.

The next game was a blowout. The Raptors crushed Cincinnati, so John's services were only required on one field goal attempt for forty-two yards and for kickoffs and extra points. On his way home, John stopped at a convenience store in Moonachie for some milk. He noticed a homeless man sitting outside and holding an old piece of brown cardboard on which was written, "Afghan veteran. Please help." John went in and picked up a two-quart container of milk and went to the register to pay for it. As he was paying, he asked the clerk, "Who's that outside?"

"I don't know who he is: some homeless guy, I guess." The clerk shrugged his shoulders as he answered. "I haven't seen him before."

John's conscience was now in full bloom. He had to do something. On his way out, he took a fifty-dollar bill from his wallet and gave it to the man. The man looked up. He had been looking down because many had passed him by. He expected John would be no different. But John was different. He handed the man the money, being careful to hold onto one end of the bill so the man would grasp the other end without touching John's hand. The homeless man knew what was intended and did not touch John's hand. As he took the bill he looked up, and for a split second he focused on it.

"Are you sure?" asked the homeless man, surprised that John might really intend to part with a bill of this size.

"Yes," said John. "Thank you for your service."

"Because of you I'll be able to get a room tonight," said the man. "God bless you!"

John smiled and turned to walk to his car. He felt the glow of helping someone in need.

He returned to the store the next day after practice, wondering if the man would still be there, but he was gone. *I wonder if I did enough*, John thought to himself.

As the games continued, John received increasing insults and criticisms from his nemesis, Harvey. But Harvey's ire had a new focus. It had become John's practice to pray the rosary on the sidelines while the game progressed. He had started the practice early, but by now all had noticed it. Why did he do this? In a secular, rational society, public displays of religion outside of church were unusual, if not considered fully inappropriate, and such practices would generally bring opprobrium. The crowd is fickle, and although John was doing a good job as a kicker, his breaking from the norms of the group was an intolerable problem. Didn't he know how to act? Harvey was particularly annoyed. John should be focusing on the game, Harvey felt. The team, and especially Harvey, had worked hard and sweated, and everyone should pay attention. When Harvey left the field, after talking on the sidelines to the defensive line coach for some game pointers, he walked over to where John was standing and said in a low but determined voice, "What are you doing? You should be watching the game and rooting for your teammates. Pray when you're in church."

John only smiled briefly and then returned to his prayers. Harvey shook his head and turned and walked away. This was a football team, and John should know how to act, he felt. He would straighten him out in the locker room. Accordingly, after the game, when the players were in the locker room, Harvey walked over to John's locker and in an angry tone yelled at John, "What's wrong with you, man? Can't you pay attention during games and root for your teammates?" But John only turned and smiled. He absorbed the complaint, but it was clear that it rolled off his back as if nothing had been said. John turned back to his locker.

Now Harvey was frustrated that his complaint had no effect and pushed John in the back, sending him careening into the locker in front of him. The other teammates had just been watching. Some watched overtly, and some hid their observance behind other tasks, such as removing their shoes or equipment, but most knew what was happening. Opinion was divided, but now Harvey had gone too far. To coldcock John in the back like that could not be tolerated. Several teammates rushed over and restrained Harvey, but clearly things had escalated. As they held Harvey back, he became more and more frustrated, resulting in his venting a foulmouthed tirade in John's direction.

John picked himself up, gathered himself, grabbed his things, and left the locker room. He drove to the convenience store for cup of coffee, and there was the homeless man outside the store again. John saw him right away. Many had passed him by as if he didn't exist. John did not pass him by. Instead he knelt down in front of him.

"What's your name?" John asked.

"My name is Frank Hawkins," the man answered.

"Why are you here?" John asked.

"I got fired from my job, and I couldn't pay my rent."

"Are you all alone in life? Is there no one to take care of you?"

"No one."

35

"How old are you?"

"I'm thirty-six."

"What did you do in Afghanistan?" John asked.

"I did two tours in Afghanistan. When I got out I couldn't find work for six months, but I finally got a job as an accountant at a construction company. But they downsized, and I was terminated. I looked all over, but I couldn't find anything else. My unemployment wasn't enough to pay my rent, and eventually that ran out too. I lost my apartment, and I had no place to go. I tried the shelters, but they were dangerous. I went there once, but I got beat up, and most of my things were stolen. I've got PTSD, so I have trouble adjusting."

"Come on, get up," said John. "I'm going to help you."

"Where are we going?" Frank asked.

"We're going to see a friend of mine," said John. They got into John's car. John took out his cell phone and dialed the number.

"Hello," said a woman's voice.

"Sister, it's John. I need your help."

"What can I do to help?" asked Sister Francis with some urgency and concern in her voice.

"I have a fellow serviceman with me who has no home and no job. I found him outside the convenience store. He needs help, Sister."

"Bring him here," said Sister. John did as Sister asked, and Sister embraced Frank and hugged him. She fed him and found a place for him to spend the night. The next day she arranged for him to take a shower and wash his clothes. They were too shabby to suit her. She then drove him to Walmart, where she bought him new underwear, socks, a pair of black slacks, and a shirt. She figured black would be the best color for the pants so they wouldn't show any dirt. She then told him to get dressed in the new clothes and, after he finished, drove him to see a former student of hers who owned three McDonald's restaurant franchises. There she put the arm on her former student to give Frank a job and let him sleep in the back on a cot until she could find him a room to rent, which she promptly did. She negotiated down the rent at a somewhat rundown but clean extra room in a house owned by an old parishioner in Paterson who was eighty-six years young and who Sister visited twice a week to bring groceries and do errands.

John did his part and got tickets for Sister and Frank to watch the next game from the sidelines. Now three people were praying the rosary on the sidelines between John's three field goals and kickoffs. Frank had no chance escaping Sister's grasp. He had been a fallen-away Catholic, but Sister would see to remedying that too. She would not neglect the soul to take care of the body. She was a marvel, and John, for his part, was happy to help them both.

Long before contracting leukemia, Sister had been frail in her youth; she had once gotten pneumonia and almost died. She spent many weeks in bed and had been constantly nursed by her mother, who prayed the rosary for the return of Sister's health. She did recover, but her lung function never completely returned, a reminder from God of her own limitations and of the need to continue the rosary. She got into track and football in an effort to reinvigorate herself and to build up stamina. She often thought of the blessings of that illness and its fruits, and how it had led her to the rosary and to becoming a nun. What seemed like the worst had become the best. Sister believed that the rosary had saved her, so she started to use it to save others. John had been one of them. The rosary was a lifeline she had thrown to him, and he had grasped it and never let go.

Of course, Harvey, his teammates, and the coaches noticed three people saying the rosary on the sidelines. The coaches had noticed John praying before, but the head coach was a graduate of Notre Dame, where he had been a starting guard, and he let it be known that as long as John made his kicks, no one was to bother him. Indeed, one day at practice he wandered over to John and whispered, "Say a prayer for me." John nodded.

Frank loved the game, as did Sister. They attended the next game as well. Same scene. Same result. John kicked two field goals. Harvey was completely outclassed. He was still frustrated, but he knew better than to take on a nun. No one on the team would have tolerated it. He snarled but kept his mouth shut.

As time went on, John became a favorite of the trainers and others at the stadium. He stopped and talked to all he passed. He had time for them all. He brought a smile to their faces. He tried to be a friend to all. He would be quick with a smile or a joke. He was the kind of man who clearly would help you if he could.

The next game was tough and hard fought against Pittsburgh. John made two field goals, but on the third, from fifty yards, the holder did not get a good plant on the ball, causing John to pull it to the left. It was the first field goal he had missed. It wasn't his fault, but a miss is a miss. Excuses would not be appreciated. As a Marine, John had been through worse. Still, he could feel the chill as he returned to the sidelines.

That was not the only tragedy of the game. Harvey had been putting pressure on the quarterback throughout the game. Finally, in the third quarter, the Pittsburgh fullback hit Harvey at his right knee, and Harvey was injured on the play. After the doctor and trainer came out on the field, Harvey was helped to the sidelines and taken back for X-rays, which showed damage to the tendons in his right knee. He needed an operation and would be out for the rest of the season. That would be a real loss. Harvey was obnoxious and arrogant, but he was an aggressive defensive end who had already racked up ten sacks. His replacement was a rookie and a good player but nothing like Harvey.

The team had been staying in the hunt to make the playoffs but was only one game ahead of New England in the race to win the division and have home field advantage. There were only a few games left in the season. The challenge for John was as much off the field as on. Harvey was injured, and John needed to do something. John prayed over it, and it came to him to go visit Sister Francis to get her advice. She would know what to do.

John went to see her. "Sister, a teammate of mine blew out his knee. I'd like to go visit him, but it's complicated." John looked at Sister for the answer, but as he did so Sister said nothing. She just waited. Her silence beckoned John to say more.

"I don't think he likes me. He's been my nemesis on the team. He insults me and criticizes me all the time. I'm afraid he might reject my overtures."

"John, what's wrong with you? You're a Marine and a Christian. Don't think about yourself. Think only of him and what he needs. Don't worry about anything else. Go to him and help him. Don't let any negative thoughts deter you."

John followed her advice, and he didn't get the warmest reception. It wasn't just that Harvey didn't like John. Harvey was so far into himself and his problem that he had neither the time nor the inclination to open up to anyone else. Still, John had gone to see him. He had taken the first step and planted the seed. Maybe something would grow from it.

John left the hospital and just walked for a while. It wasn't as if he had any great thoughts. He just felt sad. He couldn't get through to Harvey. What had he accomplished? He'd even missed his last field goal. He just felt bummed. He longed to do more, to be more, to be part of something more. He thought maybe football would give him what the

Marines had given him, a sense of being part of something bigger than himself and a sense of clear purpose. But he was only a kicker. He did not make many friends on the team. Even the punter seemed a little distant. Perhaps he was embarrassed that John knew about his son's problems or perhaps he just didn't know how to respond to John. Many people don't know how to be grateful over the long term. Sometimes they just don't know how to act or are embarrassed or don't like being in someone's debt or feeling obligated. Or was maybe John just imagining the whole thing? John was a good man, but he had doubts like everyone else. He longed to belong, to accomplish, to matter, and to succeed. He prayed and prayed, and finally it came to him. He was part of something greater. How could he be so stupid and not realize it? God would forgive his weak faith, he was sure. God's mercy is endless. He knew it was true. He smiled. For the moment, his self-pity was over.

5

THE PLAYOFF RUN

It was now time to make the final run for the playoffs. For John, the run would be different than for the others. The team wanted to make the playoffs. John wanted that too, but he wanted more. He wanted to matter. He wanted to find a purpose for himself more than he wanted any titles. He wanted to find his way. He would try to put as much effort into the race for his life as the team would put into the race for the playoffs. He was now focused, and he kept reminding himself that he was a Marine. He would adapt. He would overcome.

The next day, John put everything he had into his practice. He started at the forty-yard line and kicked field goals every five yards up to the seventy-yard line. He missed wide left at seventy yards, but he kept at it. He practiced more and more kicks until he finally made it consistently. The following day he did the same thing. And the day after he did the same—on and on, day after day. He had learned from his leg to keep at it and never quit. Gradually, he improved consistency. His determination and focus were intense. All could sense it. Something had come over him. He had been a good kicker, but now it was as if he was on a mission.

He visited Harvey every day after practice. Harvey was still an obnoxious grouch who was completely self-absorbed, but John did not let that deter him. He would bring cookies, gum, newspapers, magazines, anything. He did everything he could to reach Harvey, but based on appearances, nothing got through. The truth was that

Harvey was a jerk, but John didn't see it or didn't care. Others on the team visited and could see it too. No one understood how John could stand it. John seemed unfazed.

John also visited Sister Francis frequently, and they would go to eat at the McDonald's where Frank worked. Frank was behind the counter, but he'd put on a big smile when they came. Sister ordered a salad with strips of chicken. John had a Quarter Pounder with cheese, fries, and a big soda. He needed energy to win the race. He seemed happy. For then, at least, he had found a purpose.

On some nights John would eat dinner at the local diner, but as a treat one Friday night he decided to stop by a little Italian restaurant, a small family place in Paterson that had a reputation for good food. When the waitress came up to his table, he looked up and recognized her: a high school classmate named Susan. She was tall, about five foot eight inches, with brown hair and green eyes. She was slender and pretty. She recognized John as well and put on a big smile.

"Hello, Susan. It's good to see you! It's been a while."

"It has been a while, John. Where have you been keeping yourself?" Susan asked.

"I was in the Marines until recently. In Afghanistan."

"How was it?"

"Pretty rough. I try not to focus on it too much."

"What are you up to now?" asked Susan.

"I'm playing for the Raptors. I'm the kicker. Did you see me on TV?"

"I'm sorry," said Susan smiling. "I don't follow football."

"Well, maybe we can change that. You look great, Susan. How have you been?"

"I've been fine. I wanted to go to college, but we didn't have the money, so I work here in my father's restaurant and take courses at night at the local community college."

"That's great!" said John. "It's great to see you, Susan!"

"Well, what do you want for dinner?" Susan asked with a laugh and a tilt of her head. She handed John a menu.

John ordered chicken Parmesan over linguine with a glass of Cabernet. The meal was great, but his focus was on Susan. He liked her a lot. He noticed she did not wear a wedding ring, and Susan noticed the same about John. But there was a problem he would have to deal with, the wound he had sustained in Afganistan. After he finished the main course, Susan came back with the dessert menu. John declined desert but ordered a cup of coffee. When Susan brought the coffee, John looked up and said, "Susan, the food was great, and it's great to see you again. I lost my mother while I was deployed, and I've been lonely. It's great to see an old friend again!"

"It was great to see you too, John. Don't be a stranger," Susan said with a big smile.

"Maybe we could get together for dinner sometime? Even better, why don't you come see me play in a game?" John asked with an equally big smile on his face. He was broad in the shoulders and had a quiet strength about him. He carried himself as a military man would. He had a beautiful smile, with large white teeth and a glow in his eyes. Susan felt attracted, and the fact he was a bad boy in high school and a Marine only increased the attraction. The feeling was clearly mutual.

"Okay. I don't know much about football, but I'd love to go."

"Okay, then," said John. "I'll bring a ticket for you next week, and you can attend the game the next Sunday we're playing at home."

"Great!" said Susan, showing her big smile again.

"Great!" said John. "I'll see you next Friday with the ticket. Have a great week!" Susan handed John the bill. As he got up, he leaned over and gave Susan a kiss on the cheek. She smiled and appeared to love it.

"See you next week, Susan! Take care!" With that John left.

As John left the restaurant he had a certain glow about him. Then a feeling of sadness came over him. How would Susan take the news? He had been wounded during his deployment, which is what led to his leaving the Marines. John had been out on patrol and wound up in a firefight in which he was shot in the right leg. The bullet went through his leg and hit his groin, causing significant damage. John was discharged with a disability; the doctor said he could not have children in the normal way as a result of the wound. The doctors could harvest his sperm, but his normal function was impaired. John had not fully faced his disability, but he liked Susan and would have to face it—but not that night. He would focus on it the next day.

The next game was on the road. John kicked a fifty-two-yard field goal as well as a forty-three yarder. By now his reputation was growing, and the coaches and players recognized his talents. Even the television commentators were taking notice as his statistics built up. After the game, a female commentator on the sidelines even interviewed him for a moment. The fact that John had been a Marine, didn't play in college, and yet had great results made an interesting storyline, and his open smile combined with his quiet strength, military bearing, and humble mannerisms made him a natural hit. The commentators liked him right off. With Harvey sidelined with an injury, John's teammates were also warming up.

John attended mass every Saturday night because Sunday was game day. He would often stop at a church during the week when he could.

Many athletes credited their own abilities and talents for their success, but John gave constant thanks and praise to God for his success as well as for his suffering. All things work together for good for those who trust God. John believed this in his soul. That did not mean he didn't feel his trials and suffering. He had worried before about his wound and how it would affect his life. Like so many wounds, his was an unseen wound that worked as much on his mind as on his body. The temptation for doubt and self-pity crept in even more. How would this affect his ability to have a relationship with Susan or with any other woman for that matter? He really liked Susan, and he could tell she liked him. "Please God," he would pray, "help me with Susan. Help me find my way."

As has been said, the prayers of the righteous who obey and trust in God pierce the clouds and do not return until they have accomplished their purpose. John's prayer would be answered but not in a way foreseen by humankind.

Susan attended the next game. John was able to get her a ticket in the lower deck but above the tenth row, so she was elevated enough to have a good view. She did not drink beer. She ate no stadium food. She could not see spending money at such inflated prices.

John's kickoffs all went through the end zone, and none was returned. It was as if he was showing off for Susan. He had no living relatives, but he had Sister Francis, and he hoped to have Susan. He always had his faith, of course, and that was enough. He no longer felt lonely. He felt filled with hope and love and joy.

As was his custom, John prayed the rosary on the sidelines when he was not on the field. Now that John was becoming a celebrity, the game commentators noticed and commented on it. They were respectful men and women of faith and admired John for his faith in God and his service to his country. His teammates also began to have a deep respect for John. It takes courage in this secular society to show piety.

45

There had been others who had done so and created controversy in the process. The world does not well tolerate those who don't place all their faith in secular values. So it was in John's case. Articles began to be written by secular-minded sports commentators who criticized John for praying the rosary during the games. After all, these writers noted, this was not the time or place, and further, it was odd and inappropriate. In addition, what about the rights of non-Catholics and atheists? Football was supposed to be about football. John should focus on the game and leave religion to church.

A few atheist commentators were particularly harsh in their criticism and used humor and cartoons to make fun of him. In addition, John was not married and had no obvious girlfriend. These commentators wondered what was wrong with him. But none of this deterred John. He was a Marine spiritually as well as physically. Nor did it deter Susan. In fact, she was deeply impressed. She came from an Italian family, and she respected his religion. It gave her confidence that John was grounded and was a good man. *He might even be husband material*, she thought in the distant recesses of her mind. All she knew for sure was that she liked him, and after witnessing his prayers she also admired him. To her, he was just not your typical football player. He was somehow different. He was the kind of man she had been waiting for. She decided she wanted to get to know him better, as the seeds of love are respect and admiration. In addition, he seemed easy to talk to, and he showed her respect by really listening to her. All around him seemed to like and respect him. In addition, he was handsome and athletic. He was a great catch, and she knew he liked her. She could feel it.

Susan waited for John after the game. He had kicked another two field goals of forty-two yards and forty-six yards, respectively. John took Susan out to dinner for Chinese food at a small restaurant he had picked because of the atmosphere of dim lighting and quiet tables so they could talk. They only made small talk, but the talk came easily, and John really wanted to hear what she had to say. She could open up to him, and he seemed to be opening up to her. He valued her opinion.

He respected her. The game had been at one o'clock in the afternoon, so they had gone to dinner afterward at about six o'clock and lingered there until about eight. Susan liked this guy even more and began to fantasize about him and about what being married to him would be like.

After dinner John drove to a local park, where they walked and talked for a while. It was unseasonably warm that day, so they could walk and talk without getting a chill. It had been a great day for Susan, and it ended with John taking her home by eleven o'clock. He kissed her on the cheek and wished her good night. She wanted more of a sign because she really liked him. She wondered when she could see him again.

John for his part was confused. He really liked Susan, and he was serious about finding someone to spend his life with, but he would not make a precipitous decision. Also, there was the question of that wound. "Dear Lord," he prayed, "show me the way. Help me, O Lord. "Out of the depths I call to you, Lord; Lord, hear my cry! May your ears be attentive to my cry for mercy (Psalm 130:1-2)." He also remembered the words he had seen in the chapel where he prayed after he was wounded, "In my distress I called out: Lord! I cried out to my God. From his temple he heard my voice; my cry to him reached his ears." He would trust in the Lord, for with God all things are possible.

Susan waited for a call all week, but it did not come until Thursday night.

"Hi, Susan. It's John."

"Hi, John. I was hoping you'd call."

"How about dinner Friday night after next? We're playing on the road this week, so I won't be able to see you this weekend. We're flying to Seattle tomorrow."

"I'd like that," said Susan.

47

"Great, I'll call you next week! Wish me luck with the game! Seattle has a great defense! Field goals could be key if our offense can't move the ball. To tell you the truth, I'm a little scared that I might let the team down."

She was pleased he was opening up to her.

"You won't, John. I know you. You're a good man and a Marine. You'll show them that's what you do. I'll miss you, but I will root for you. Call me. Bye."

"Bye," said John. "I'll miss you too."

Both John and Susan had a glow and basked in it as they reflected for a moment on what had transpired. But where would this relationship go, John wondered? He would have to tell her. But right now he needed to focus on the season. He would tell her after the season ended. There were only a few more games left in the regular season. They were in the hunt for the playoffs. Right now he needed to focus. Plus, he didn't know how to handle this issue. He needed more time to pray over it.

The games were getting more intense. Everyone could feel it. In the hunt for the playoffs, every game counted. Everyone was more serious, especially the coaches. Many of the players tried to stay loose by focusing on the fun of the game, but everyone realized there was a lot of money on the line. For the coaches the fun of the game was way down the list of their concerns. They were hired and paid to win. Everyone upped his game. As they moved closer to the playoffs, even the poor teams played with more intensity; players were fighting for their pride and to keep their jobs for the next year. The good teams were fighting either to win a wildcard spot or to win the division with the benefit of fewer games, possibly home field advantage, and a bigger payday.

For the kickers, the pressure was more mental. The defensive players were good on the better teams, so it would be harder for the offense to score. Also, with parity the teams were more evenly matched, so in all likelihood the games would be close. It could easily come down to a field goal to win the game. In addition to the added pressure of the playoffs, there was also the possible terrible blow to one's reputation if one cost the team the game and disappointed the fans. There wasn't much chance to be the hero or the game's MVP, but there was a great chance to be the goat if you missed the key field goal or if the kick off didn't position the ball away from a speedy and talented kick returner who, heaven forbid, could run a kickoff back all the way or give his team good field position. The mental anxiety and pressure could become intense. John was a Marine and used to combat, but there was a lot of time to think about this. Events in combat could happen quickly, with little time for forethought. Here there was plenty of time to think, and the media and the NFL did all they could to increase the pressure. They wanted to please fans by providing a lot of hype about the great contest. John needed to center himself. For that, he would see Susan. He needed her help now.

The Raptors beat Seattle. John made two field goals, but they were easy, and since the Raptors were ahead at the time, there was less pressure. Still, John knew he was lucky in the Seattle game. When the team returned home, he called Susan the next day.

"Susan, could we have dinner tonight? I'm feeling the pressure right now, and I really need someone to talk to. Besides, I miss you."

"Of course," Susan responded. "What time?"

"How about seven o'clock? I'll pick you up."

"Okay. See you then. I'm looking forward to it."

John picked Susan up that night. They headed to a quiet little Italian restaurant in Hoboken. The atmosphere was nice, the quiet would allow them to talk, and the food there was good. It was a BYOB restaurant, so John brought a bottle of chardonnay for them to share. He had made reservations, so there was no wait for the table. He wanted to get seated and share something with Susan. First, there was some very brief small talk.

"How have you been?" John asked.

"I've been great. But what about you?" Susan responded.

"Susan, I'm really feeling the pressure. I didn't think I would, but I'm worried that I'll let the team down. I don't have the experience a lot of the other kickers do. To tell you the truth, I'm scared, and I'm afraid it will affect my confidence."

Susan looked across the table at John lovingly. She just wanted to hold him, but that wouldn't work at the dinner table, so she did the next best thing. She leaned across the table and gave John a huge kiss on the lips. It was a long slow kiss. She then sat back down with a smile on her face.

She caught John by surprise. He was pleased although a little shocked. After a few seconds, he regained his composure and smiled. She had done all she needed to do. John felt happy. Down deep in his gut he was still a little scared, but all of a sudden that seemed less important. As they finished dinner, they were both very chatty. John drove Susan home after dinner and gave her a long kiss goodbye. Susan was happy. The relationship was deepening, and she felt good that she had helped him. She could just tell. John, for his part, had made up his mind. He would not fail at this. Susan was right. There are more important things than kicking field goals. But still, God gave him this chance, and he would make the most of it. He would grab it with both hands. He was a Marine. He would dig in. He would overcome.

John intensified his prayer life. He prayed the rosary each night as well as on the sidelines. He would leave his life in God's hands. He would do his best to put aside worry and to trust. The question of how to deal with the wound kept creeping into his mind, but he had enough pressure from the game.

The next game would be critical. The Raptors were playing Pittsburgh. If the Raptors won and if New England lost to Miami, the Raptors would win the division and have home field advantage and one week off before its first playoff game. This was a big game, and everyone knew it. You could feel it in practice. Everyone was focused. Everyone was stepping up his game. In the locker room there was nervous banter. The players reminded each other that this was for the division title and a big paycheck, so they urged each other on. The team announced that if the Raptors won the division there would be a dinner party that night at a local hotel. The celebrating couldn't continue for long, though, because there would be more playoff games to prepare for. However, since it had been so long since they had won the division, it would be appropriate to celebrate, at least briefly, to mark this milestone.

The game started off slowly, like two heavyweight fighters feeling each other out. Neither team could get the running game going, but they both needed to keep trying to run to open up the passing game. If either team could establish the run, it would have a balanced attack. In addition, it would be able to control the ball to prevent the other team from having the opportunity to score. Further, it could force the other team to bring the safeties up to stop the run, which would mean man-to-man coverage for the wideouts and which would allow for more opportunities in the passing game, including the possibility of a big play. But neither team could establish a solid running game. So after the first quarter, each team began to try to loosen up the defense with the passing game. The Raptors tried two long passes, hoping for either a big play or a pass interference penalty that would stretch the field and open up the offense. Both plays were unsuccessful.

Pittsburgh tried the short passing game with little success. The Raptors' linebackers were fast, so Pittsburgh's short passing game was playing into the strength of the Raptors' defense. Back and forth, back and forth: the game was a defensive struggle.

But suddenly Pittsburgh threw the ball down the field and connected on a long pass play when the Raptors' defensive back slipped and fell. The Pittsburgh receiver was tackled at the twenty-eight-yard line, but that allowed Pittsburgh deep penetration into Raptors' territory. The players couldn't move the ball any further, but the Pittsburgh kicker was able to score a field goal. He made it look easy, John thought. Oh well; John would do the same when it was his turn.

In the second quarter, Pittsburgh scored again. Its punt returner returned a punt for seventy-eight yards. Now the score was ten to zero. The Raptors still had time, but it was time to get going, and everyone knew it—especially the fans. The Raptors had to get their running game going enough to give at least some help to the passing game. Suddenly the Raptors' defense stiffened, and although Pittsburgh scored a few first downs, they couldn't move the ball in any significant way. In addition, before the half the Raptors finally scored a touchdown on a screen pass that had been well set up on the left side of the field. John kicked the extra point, so at the half the score stood at ten to seven.

During halftime both coaches decided to open up their offenses. When the teams returned to the field, the Raptors received the kickoff and drove down the field for a score. It was now fourteen to ten in favor of the Raptors. But Pittsburgh had decided to open up its offense as well. The defenses of both teams had been on the field for a long time, and they were growing tired. Scoring was now possible. Suddenly, the defensive struggle of the first half changed into an offensive shoot-out in the second half. Each team really opened up its offense and began to score. There were not only touchdowns, but the Pittsburgh kicker also scored another field goal as well. John kicked a field goal, and his kickoffs went through the end zone, so no kick returns were possible. The Raptors also scored with a few trick plays, including a halfback pass that was successful and a fake field goal that also scored. The score at the two-minute warning was tied at twenty-seven each. Then, all of a sudden, nothing seemed to work for the Raptors' offense, and

Pittsburgh found itself in the same position. Each team would now try to position itself for at least a field goal if it couldn't score a touchdown. It was time to try to get a score and win the game.

At the two-minute warning Pittsburgh had the ball on its own twenty-yard line. Pittsburgh tried two running plays but moved the ball only eight yards and then completed a short pass for six yards; the receiver was tackled in bounds, so the clock kept running. Pittsburgh moved the ball to the Raptors' side of the field but was stopped at the Raptors' forty-yard line. Try as Pittsburgh could, it could not move the ball on the first three downs. The clock ran down to twenty-five seconds. Pittsburgh now brought out its kicker, but the wind in the stadium was tricky, and the kicker's kick hit the left upright; the ball bounced off to the left. The field goal had been missed, and there was time for only one more play in regulation.

John made his way down the sidelines to the coach. The coach was about to send in the offense and play it safe, hoping to win in overtime. But John spoke up.

"Coach, I can make this." The field goal would be about seventy yards. No one would try such a thing in this situation. It was not the safe play. "Coach, you've seen me do it in practice."

"This isn't practice, John."

"Coach …" was all John said as he looked the coach straight in the eye and set his jaw. Everyone who was near knew John meant it. But still, it was crazy! What if the field goal was blocked and returned for a touchdown? What if the ball fell short and was returned for a touchdown? What if …? The coach would be laughed out of the league if he lost the game with only a few seconds left based on a crazy call like this. As the coach's mind raced he could hear the offensive coordinator yelling, "That's crazy! It's crazy!" He could see that the coach was evaluating it, and if he was evaluating it, that meant he was considering it. But something suddenly interrupted the coach's train of thought and brought his mind back to reality. It was John. His face had not moved. His teeth remained clenched. His jaw set. You could see the muscles of his jaw tighten. He looked the coach dead in the eye. He gave that Marine look.

"Coach," he repeated boldly. He said no more, but his message was clear.

"John, I can't. It's too risky."

"Coach, there's a saying in the service: 'when the going gets tough, the tough get going,' Let's go!"

Coach now looked John straight in the eye. He could see John's determination. He just stared at him. It was only a moment, but it seemed like an hour.

"Coach," a voice yelled. It was the referee. "Let's go!" *Call time-out*, the coach thought. A delay of game penalty would make any kick that much harder.

"Coach, let's go!" John said again with determination.

There was something there. Coach knew it was crazy, but yet, but yet … something was urging him to do it. Maybe they would go down, but who wants to play for second place or a tie. They say that fortune favors the bold, but relying on sayings and shibboleths is easy when someone else is making the call. He looked at John. It was as if he still had his Marine uniform on. It was absolutely crazy, but all of a sudden the coach found himself saying, "It's up to you, John. Make us proud!"

"Hoorah!" John said softly and turned to run onto the field as the field goal team was sent out.

The Pittsburgh coach and the game commentators thought the Raptors were insane. As soon as the Pittsburgh coach realized what was happening, he called a time-out to let John think about it. The fans collectively gulped. What kind of a crazy call was this? The commentators were insane at the prospect.

The field-goal team now mulled around on the field, allowing the time to run its course. John was off by himself. No one approached him. He was left alone. How often it is during any critical decision that a man is left alone. How lonely are the brave! Although there was no comparison, John considered how alone and abandoned Jesus must have felt. But then John's mind came back to the game.

John had a secret weapon. Pittsburgh had called a time-out, so John could focus on the difficult task ahead, but that is not what John started to think about. All he could think of was that kiss from Susan! A small smile crept across his face as he remembered. The commentators could not figure out how he could smile at a time like this, but it gave John quiet confidence to remember that kiss. Sure, it would be tough. A seventy-yard field goal seems almost impossible, but John remembered what his friend in Afghanistan who was a Navy seal told him the seal's motto is: "the only easy day was yesterday." But that kiss! It went through his mind again. Focusing on the kiss somehow helped to dissolve the pressure.

John now set his resolve. He whispered a prayer to the great Mother of God as he turned to look at the goalpost seventy yards away. He set his jaw again and fixed his focus. He was ready! He squared his shoulders and aligned the shot in his mind. He could see it, he could feel it, and he could almost touch it. The field-goal team members got to their positions. The defense did as well. In John's mind, he had already made the field goal.

"Hut one, hut two, hut three!" John could hear his holder calling the signals for the snap. The ball was snapped! The holder caught it. The snap was high. Everyone in the stadium held his or her breath. For John, it was as if this was happening in slow motion. The Raptors' sideline was motionless, panicking at the sight of the high snap. As the holder brought the ball down, John began his run toward the ball. As the ball was placed down, John's foot struck the ball squarely, and it was launched. It was on its way, carrying the hopes and dreams of all the Raptors and the fears of all of Pittsburgh.

The ball had been struck hard, although John did not seem to struggle with the kick or put much effort into it. It was as if the easier he kicked it, the farther the ball went. It rose high. It had been kicked well. It was high but not too high. It looked straight. It seemed to take a long time for a seventy-yard kick to reach the target. All 130,000 eyes in the stadium were on it. The eyes of the players and those on the sidelines were mesmerized. It was as if time was suspended while the ball traveled toward its target. But John did not watch. Immediately after kicking, he turned and ran toward the sidelines as if he already knew. Suddenly, a roar went up in the stadium. As he ran off the field, John suddenly saw the sidelines erupt in joy, with fans raising their hands and jumping and their faces lit with smiles as they hugged each other. John's teammates on the field looked around to see where he was to share their joy with him and congratulate him, but by now he was near the sidelines where he was mobbed by those there.

John rushed into the locker room. He avoided the reporters, changed quickly, and made his exit. A player yelled after him. It was the punter he had helped. No one was happier for John than the punter.

"Remember the party tonight, John!"

"See you there!" John yelled back.

John wanted to see Sister Francis. He had not invited Susan to the game. He was afraid he might fail and did not want her to see it. Also, he needed to focus, and if she was there he'd be distracted. As he drove to see Sister Francis, he called Susan on his cell phone. She answered the phone enthusiastically.

"Congratulations, John! You were great! What a kick! I knew you could do it! They're all talking about it!"

"There's a dinner tonight to celebrate. I'd like you to come with me!"

"Of course, but I need to get dressed." Susan was all smiles on the phone. "What should I wear?"

"Get dressed up, honey. I'll pick you up at six thirty. See you then!"

John continued on his way to see Sister Francis. When he arrived, he rang the bell, and Sister answered. She had not watched the game. She did not know about his kick. She would, of course, be happy for him, but he was looking for something else. When he saw her he fell to his knees in front of her.

"Sister, I need your help." Sister leaned forward and grasped his head in her hands.

"Of course, my son. How can I help you?"

"I need to give thanks, Sister. I … I just received a gift from God. He helped me kick a seventy-yard field goal. I have less experience than anyone else in the league. I never went to college, but he gave me this gift. And something else also. I met a wonderful girl, Sister. You know about my wound. I need to ask God to help me with her." John told Sister all about Susan, where she lived, and how much he cared for her.

"John, John, John! Just turn back to Jesus with all your heart. He will hear your prayer of thanks, and He will help you with this girl. Come in. I have something I want to give you that will help."

John followed her into the convent foyer. "Wait here," said Sister. "I'll be right back." Sister disappeared for a few minutes and returned with a new rosary contained in a blue imitation leather case. John unzipped the case and took out the new rosary.

"It's a new Lourdes rosary. It has already been blessed. Use this to say your thanks. Each day as you meditate on the mysteries of the rosary and on the events in the life of Christ, make the virtues you find there your own. Occupy yourself with His interests, and He will occupy Himself with yours. I put a little note into the rosary case. Don't read it until you get home. Now go! I will pray for you." John thanked Sister Francis and gave her a hug. If she had given him the world it would not have meant so much.

He then went to pick up Susan. He had plenty of time, so he did not take the main roads but opted to take the side streets so he could think and reflect and soak in the joy of the moment. He spotted a local pharmacy and pulled into the rather large parking lot to get a package of mints. As he exited the store, he saw a man pushing and shoving a woman. The man was trying to carjack the car, a recent model BMW. John did not hesitate, but when he got there and spun the man around, the man plunged a knife into John's chest just below his sternum. John's eyes popped wide, and he slumped to the ground. The woman screamed. The man ran off. The woman ran screaming and crying into the store.

"Call the police! Call the police! Someone's been stabbed!" she yelled and sobbed at the same time.

The police came, but John was dead. They did not know who he was, so they searched his pockets and found the rosary case and his driver's license. They had been on duty, so they did not know about John's seventy-yard kick. They did not know his next of kin, but they found the note from Sister Francis. The policeman opened it and read it. "Always remember that God loves you. Place all your trust in Him." It was signed, "Love, Sister Francis."

The policeman who searched John's body knew Sister Francis. He did not want to just call her. Her residence was not that far away. He would go visit her and break the news in person. She deserved that courtesy and much more. She had given years of selfless service to others, and the policeman knew it. So it came to pass that he and his partner drove to see Sister Francis and knocked on the door.

"Hello, Sister."

"Officer Ryan. What can I do for you?"

"I have some bad news, Sister. Do you know a young man named John Thaddeus?"

"Yes, I do," Sister replied, but her tone indicated she knew bad news was about to come. The anticipation of tragedy showed on her face.

"Well, I'm sorry to tell you this. He was killed just a while ago. We found your note in his rosary case, so I thought I would check with you about him."

"Oh no!" exclaimed Sister Francis. "Why? Where did this happen? I just talked to him a little while ago! He is the kicker for the Raptors."

"I thought his name sounded familiar. He apparently tried to stop a carjacking in the parking lot of the pharmacy on Houston Street. The man was attempting to push a woman into the car. He ran to help, and the man stabbed him. We have an APB out for the perp now."

"Oh no!" exclaimed Sister Francis with tears welling up in her eyes.

"Sister, did he have any next of kin? We should notify them," the policeman asked.

"No, he's all alone, but he did tell me about a girl he was dating. Her name is Susan LaCava. I don't know her address, but she works at her father's restaurant in Paterson," said Sister Francis.

"We can get the address," said the policeman.

"Do you want me to be the one to tell her, officer?" asked Sister.

"I'd appreciate that," said the officer. "Hold on; I'll get you her address." The officer did as he promised. He had his partner call the precinct and asked them to get the address and the phone number and then returned and gave them to Sister Francis. Sister said goodbye to the officer and closed the door. She paused for a moment to say a silent prayer for John, but she was anxious to call Susan before Susan could hear it from another source. First she wanted guidance. She had seen much death in her time as a nun but never murder, especially of someone so young and so close to her. The need to move quickly to tell Susan distracted her from her overwhelming sorrow and grief. She decided to visit the chapel in the nun's residence for a brief prayer for guidance and help before she made the call. She did so and prayed to God to receive John's soul, to forgive him any transgressions, and to care for him. She also prayed for help and guidance in dealing with Susan. The visit in the chapel was brief. It does not take long to open one's heart to God.

Sister then walked to her small cell in the residence where she had a phone. She dialed Susan's cell phone number. A young woman's voice answered.

"Susan, my name is Sister Francis. I'm a friend of John Thaddeus. I know you and he were seeing each other. I have some bad news. John has died!"

Before Sister could finish, Susan broke into hysterical crying. Sister could hear the sobbing and could feel Susan's pain.

After the initial explosion of Susan's grief, she composed herself enough, though barely, to ask, "How did he die? He was supposed to pick me up to take me to a dinner with his team tonight. I don't understand! Could you be mistaken?" she asked with hope.

Denial is often the first phase of mourning.

"John tried to stop the carjacking of a woman in the pharmacy parking lot, and he was stabbed," said Sister.

"How did you find out? When did this happen?" Susan asked.

"John had a note from me on him, and that lead a policeman, Officer Ryan, whom I knew, to come to me and ask whom he should notify. You know that John didn't have any family, but he told me that you and he were dating. I asked Officer Ryan if I could be the one to notify you rather than having you get a call or a visit from the police."

Sister could hear more sobbing over the phone as she continued. "You know John was a Marine, and he would never see someone who needed help and not help."

Again there was more sobbing and outright crying. Sister continued.

"I've known John for many years, and I have always loved him. He was a wonderful young man! He got his life together and was just starting to really do and be something. I will miss him greatly."

"Oh, Sister! How can I deal with this? We have not been dating for long. I knew John from high school, before he joined the Marines. But when he came back ..." There was more crying and heavy sobbing as Susan paused for a moment.

"I prayed for John for years, even before he went into the Marines and, of course, for his safe return what he was deployed. But now we must pray to him to help us deal with this loss. I have something I think he would want you to have," said Sister.

"What is it, Sister?" asked Susan.

"It's the new rosary I gave John. Officer Ryan returned it to me. The rosary helped John turn his life around, and it has helped me too. I think he would tell you, if he were here, that it was his most prized possession, because for every day of the week and every circumstance in life it recalls an event in the life of Jesus that exhibited a virtue that can help you. I assure you, there is no problem in life that cannot be solved at the foot of the cross and in the mysteries of the rosary. I know he would like you to have it. When you pray it, pray it for him."

"Thank you, Sister. Let me have your phone number and address, and I'll make an appointment to pick it up."

By now Susan's mind began to return to normal, if only briefly, and she remembered the team dinner. "Sister, John was going to take me to a dinner tonight to celebrate the team's victory today and winning the division. Someone needs to notify them. I don't think I can do it. I'm just too upset. I don't have their phone number. Someone needs to go to the hotel to tell them."

"All right, Susan; I will go. You rest, and if you need someone to talk to, I'm here. I'll give you my phone number and address. What hotel is the dinner at?"

Susan told Sister Francis the dinner was at the Hilton Hotel ballroom in Parsippany at seven o'clock. By now it was around six o'clock, so there was not much time to talk to the coach in advance of the dinner.

"I'll leave right away," said Sister.

Sister got her coat since it was December and the sun had gone down. Her coat was black and plain. Sister Francis, then more advanced in age than when John had first met her, had returned to wearing a habit. Since she needed to leave quickly, there was no time to change. Her habit was worn and had been carefully mended in various spots, but it was meticulously clean. Indeed, to her, it was the finest garment in the world. Sister only owned one other habit to be used when this one was soiled. Sister's habit was an outward sign that she had clothed herself with the garb of penance and contrition. But her sacrifice was far more meaningful and important than the sacrifice of worldly possessions.

Her sacrifice was a contrite heart. She rendered her heart, not her garments. Whenever someone would see her helping the poor, they'd recall an image from two thousand years before. When she cared for others, it was as if she held in her arms the crucified Jesus—who, after having been taken down from the cross, rested in his mother's arms.

Sister arrived at the Hilton at about seven-thirty. She parked in a full lot at the side of the hotel. She had never used valet. She walked slowly toward the main entrance and made her way to the front desk.

"Excuse me, sir. Can you please tell me where the Raptors' dinner is?" asked Sister.

"Are you a guest, Sister? It's a private affair," said the clerk.

"I'm not attending the dinner. I have a message for the coach," said Sister.

"Okay, Sister. Just follow this hallway to the end and make a right, and you'll see the main ballroom where they are," said the clerk. "You'll have to clear their security people to be admitted."

"Thank you," said Sister. She now walked slowly and prayerfully as if carrying the cross. She knew this would not be easy. She prayed, "Jesus, I trust in you."

She turned right at the end of the hall and could hear the joyous merriment of the players. She explained her purpose to the security people who guarded the room. The doors to the room were closed and heavy; she struggled to open one, and the security guard quickly helped her with the door.. She stepped inside the room and stood there for a moment as she looked around. Finally, one of the assistant coaches came up to her. He had a drink in his hand and was dressed in a sports coat and slacks with a nicely pressed shirt and tie.

"Can I help you, Sister?" he asked.

"Yes, please. I have something I need to discuss with the head coach," she said.

"Let me show you where he is, Sister. He's upfront."

They made their way up the aisle between tables and approached the head coach, a man in his fifties, who was all smiles and who also had a drink in his hands.

"Coach, Sister said she needs to talk to you," the assistant coach said. It was the same assistant John had met so long ago. After introducing Sister Francis, he stood to listen. The group included the coach and his wife and various assistant coaches and their wives.

"What can I do for you, Sister?" the coach asked. He was all smiles. He must have felt that nothing could have dulled the joy of that moment. Winning the division meant the coach's job was secure, and he also felt the joy that comes from such a team achievement.

"I am Sister Francis, and I am afraid I have some bad news, sir. John Thaddeus has been killed trying to protect a woman who was being carjacked today after the game."

The news hit the group like a bomb. For a moment, the group hung there in disbelief. Then the coach finally spoke.

"Sister, are you sure you have the right guy? John was the hero of the game today. We only finished playing at four o'clock this afternoon."

All present knew in their gut there was no mistake. The coach's query was almost a reflexive question, because the shock of the news had momentarily robbed everyone of all reason and grace.

"Yes, sir, I'm sorry to say. The police came to see me, because they found a note from me in John's pocket. I notified his girlfriend, and she asked me to tell you."

The shock of the news spread out from the small group like a tidal wave. You could almost see and feel the wave spread to the far reaches of the rather large room. The coach signaled the band to stop playing. He walked slowly to the microphone. He put his drink down on a table. All joy now went out of his face. He took a moment to compose himself.

"I have just received some very bad news. John Thaddeus has been killed. He died trying to protect a woman from a carjacking. I just received the news from Sister Francis." The room shuttered. Moans and muffled groans of "Oh no!" and "That's awful!" could be heard. All merriment stopped. Most put down their drinks. The wives looked around, not sure how to act. A few sobs could be heard from somewhere in the room. The coach asked for a moment of silence for John.

Harvey now made his way through the crowd. Guilt had overcome him. It does not take long for that to happen, especially for a team leader with sudden remorse.

"Sister, my name is Harvey Johnson. How did this happen?" Sister recounted what she knew. A tear rolled down Harvey's left cheek. He did not wipe it away. He extended his hand for Sister to shake, and she did so.

"Did he have any family, Sister?" Harvey asked.

"Only all of us here," said Sister. More tears began.

"You know, Sister, I gave him a hard time. He would always pray on the sidelines, and I thought he should be more focused on the game." He said this hoping that Sister could give him absolution. "I guess he was praying for victory," said Harvey.

"No," said Sister Francis. "Didn't you know? He was praying for you." Now Harvey really began to cry. The truth can cut like a knife.

Sister said goodbye to the coach and the small group and walked slowly to make her exit. It was as if John's life left with her.

The next day the media was all abuzz about John's fate. He'd been a player in the NFL, a Marine, and the hero of the last game. This made for a great story in their eyes. They interviewed the coach and some players, but it was the punter who was the most willing to be interviewed and who provided the greatest insight into John. A representative of the media caught him on his way to the locker room from practice.

"John was a terrific guy. He was new to the team, so many did not really know him, but I knew him. We were both kickers. He would help anyone who needed help. I'm not surprised he tried to help a woman being carjacked. I would have been surprised if he hadn't. He was my friend, and about my friend I will only say this—there was present in him all the virtues of humility, piety, patient endurance, faith, hope, charity, courage, and the love of God. I loved him, and he loved me. I will miss him terribly. Now I will pray to him to intercede for me and my family and to continue to help us from the next life as he did in this life."

With that he walked away and did not grant any further interviews.

The team called back the last kicker who had tried out for the team so many months before. There was another game to play in two weeks. Life moves on even when an individual life does not. Most of the players had not gotten to know John well; they felt bad, but he was not the emotional center of the team. Harvey felt some guilt about how he had treated John but not overly so. He was too focused on himself to turn his gaze outward to another for very long. He resolved not to think about it anymore. There was the rest of the season to focus on. How quickly the departed can be forgotten! How short is the memory of the living! Only God remembers the lives of those who have fallen asleep. How many saints are known only to God?

The funeral mass for John was held on Monday, which is the team's day off, so most who wanted to could attend. The priest who said the funeral mass had asked Sister Francis if she would say a few words since he knew she'd had a special relationship with John. She agreed, but she was too humble to call it a eulogy; the way she thought of it, she was just going to say a few words for her friend. She would spend many hours praying to God for the repose of John's soul. She was sad for John, but she believed he was in God's hands.

It was a sunny morning on the day of the funeral, which was held at St. Anne's Church in Hoboken because John had made donations and felt close to the Capuchin Friars of St. Francis who staff that church. Sister Francis knew them well. After all, she had chosen "Francis" as her religious name and had attended many retreats and masses said by Capuchin friars.

The service was crowded. Most of the team attended as well as a few members of the press. Susan was also there. The service was beautiful. The concluding portion of the mass contained the final commendation, including the beautiful song of farewell.

At the end of the service, the priest sat down on a large chair off to the side of the altar, and Sister Francis slowly made her way to the pulpit. Her slow gait made it seem as if she carried the cross on her slim shoulders as she climbed the three steps to the level upon which the pulpit was placed. When she arrived at the pulpit she climbed another two steps and reached up to adjust the microphone, pulling it down because she was only five feet four inches tall. She looked down from the elevated pulpit and across the ample audience. She smiled briefly and then began.

"If you stand on the corner of Times Square and Forty-Second Street and travel eighteen miles northwest, you come to the town of Paterson, where John grew up. For a while, he lived in a house on a corner lot, and he would tell me that the house was so situated that when he looked out the kitchen window he looked across the backyards of all the houses on the perpendicular block. That house was modest, but looking out that window across all the fenceless backyards was as if he was looking out at a beautiful park, lush in its green hue. Now if God can clothe in such beauty this place of our exile, what must paradise be like and, even more, the face of God? We must honor John's memory, because I believe that even now he may be looking upon the face of God. Although we will miss him, and I miss him terribly, my sorrow is tempered by his newfound joy, which no one will take from him."

Sister paused for a moment before continuing.

"John did not have an easy life. He was in and out of trouble as a youth, which is when I first got to know him. He went into the Marines to straighten himself out. But God sometimes chases a man, and so it was with John. Many of you may not know this, but John was wounded while in combat. There is no progress aside from the cross, and John learned to bear his cross patiently and with resignation. He was tested and formed by his suffering. The cross can either crush a man or lift him up and be redemptive. For John, it was the latter. He learned to focus not on himself and his problems but on the problems and needs of others, and from his suffering he learned to turn back to God and to trust in Him. There he found how to be redeemed by his sufferings; he united them to the sufferings of Jesus by which all people have been redeemed.

"As I mentioned, John's path was not an easy one. He was also wounded spiritually. He had killed men, and he bore a level of guilt that he did not share with many. Some who have returned from war, where they have seen and done horrible things, think it is too late for them to be saved. But, as John's life proves, it is never too late. Such is the great mercy of God, if we will only trust in His mercy. I tell you this because there may be some in this audience who may be thinking it is too late for them or who think they cannot be saved or, worse yet, have not even considered their souls and their fates. Maybe there are those here who are walking through life with apathy about their paths to God. When you think of John, realize he was more wounded than many of you. Believe me, I know. He had a difficult path, but as a result of all he had been through he was without guile, and he died helping others.

"As John came to learn, the best path back to God is through prayer and trust in His mercy. John prayed the rosary. Each decade focuses on a different event in the life of Jesus and a different virtue upon which to model our lives. John knew that to reach God we must imitate Christ, and the rosary shows us the virtues to imitate. The rosary is a lifeline dropped down from heaven, which, if we grasp it, will pull us up out of the events of this world and into the life of Christ. John came to know this, and by his life he showed it to all of us."

Sister paused and looked down for a moment. Then she continued.

"I have talked a little about John's life. But what are we to make of John's death? The message, my brothers and sisters, is that nothing else matters if you do not come to know Jesus Christ and trust in His unfathomable mercy. And more, we must be ready every day. None of us knows the hour of our death. Let John's death be a message to us, his final gift to us. Be prepared. Get ready. Get rid of apathy. As John's life demonstrates, the time is short, and the night will shortly be upon us.

"But as we reflect on the violent way John died, should we be afraid to help others for fear we might meet the same fate as John? To that I will repeat the same words that I told John when I wrote to him in Afghanistan when he was afraid: 'You shall not fear the terror of the night nor the arrow that flies by day (Psalm 91:5NABRE).' Even if you should die, He will raise you up.

"But what if, like John, you carry the burden of guilt or other problems? I recently read in the newspaper that scientists have discovered a star billions of light-years away. Just imagine: billions of light-years away! How great and vast is God's creation, and as vast as it is, even greater and vaster is the mercy of God to those who call upon Him. His mercy is available especially at three o'clock, the great hour of mercy. Learn a lesson then from the sights people see in the heavens—the distant stars and wonders. Even more wondrous and vast is the mercy of God to all who trust in His mercy. Like John, may we trust in God's mercy to overcome the obstacles in our paths and help us find our ways to God as John did. John, thank you for this lesson that you have left us. We will pray for you. Please pray for us."

Sister Francis turned away and looked down at the steps of the pulpit so as not to lose her footing. She walked slowly back to her seat. The priest stood and walked toward the casket. The funeral then concluded with a hymn that included the same words from the Psalm: "You shall not fear the terror of the night nor the arrow that flies by day (Psalm 91:5 NABRE)."

The priest walked around the casket, blessing it with holy water, and then stood in front of the altar. After the concluding prayer, the choir sang another beautiful hymn while the coffin was led down the aisle.

Six pallbearers, teammates who had been lined up by the team's punter, lifted the casket into the hearse. There were not enough flowers for a separate floral car, so all the flowers were placed in the same hearse.

John was interred at a local cemetery in hallowed ground. Down through the years his grave had three regular visitors: Susan, the punter, and Sister Francis, when she was able or could get a ride, although she honored John more with her prayers than her graveside visits.

One day, not long after the funeral, there was a knock at the door of the convent where Sister Francis lived. Sister Francis was summoned to meet a guest. It was Susan.

"Hello, Sister. I'm Susan LaCava. I came to pick up John Thaddeus's rosary. I was driving by and took a chance you would be in."

"Come in, come in, Susan. Have a seat. I'll go get it." Sister now went to her small cell to get the rosary, and when she returned she extended her hand to give it to Susan.

"Here you are, Susan. This meant a lot to John. It is his gift to you now! The rosary saw him through a lot of tough times—more than you know. It can do the same for you." Sister paused as she handed Susan the rosary. "How have you been, Susan?" Sister asked as she sought to look Susan in the eye. Susan raised her glance from the rosary and stared at Sister Francis. Her eyes welled up, and she began to cry.

"Sit, sit," Sister said. Susan had stood up to receive the rosary, so Susan sat back down and lowered her head as she cried to hide at least a little of her emotions.

"Sister, sometimes, I don't know, I just feel so lost, so sad. I really liked John. We hadn't dated for long but I thought … I guess I thought, I don't know …"

"You thought maybe he was the one, Susan?" Sister asked.

"I guess so. I don't know," Susan answered. "I don't understand. I've always gone to church, but I don't understand how God can allow this to happen."

"Susan, look at me," Sister said. She had seen much suffering, but it had strengthened her faith rather than weakened it. Sister grasped Susan's hands, which still held the rosary. With a compassionate face that only an old, tired nun can provide, she lowered her voice, and she looked into Susan's eyes. "Humankind has wrestled with the problem of suffering since before the time of Job. The whole story of Job is a story of the human effort to understand the meaning of suffering. Job had everything and was blameless and righteous. He was wealthy and had a family, but the devil told God that Job was only loyal because he had been blessed. So the devil tested Job by taking it all away. I've seen it happen many times. Evil can try to destroy a life.

71

"Three supposed wise friends of Job showed up and tried to explain the suffering. To them, Job must have sinned and offended God. But Job did not believe them. He knew he had always been righteous. Job's wife despaired and told Job to curse God and die. But Job would not. Instead he remains faithful and says that if we are willing to receive the good things from God, we should also be willing to accept the bad. He says that "The Lord gave and the Lord has taken away; blessed be the name of the Lord! (Job 1:21)." He realizes that through it all we need to maintain our faith in God and bless His name despite whatever challenges come our way. We must always keep our faith. Job also realizes that his redeemer lives and that he will see God from his own body someday.

"Job was right. We cannot fully explain why bad things happen to good people. The three wise friends are a symbol of humankind trying to explain the meaning of the righteous having to endure suffering. The lesson of Job is that we cannot fully grasp God's plans, but in the end God will reward us. Our only answer can be trust in God, who made heaven and earth.

"The New Testament finally gives us the answer to the question of suffering that is raised in the story of Job. Job saw that the answer is faith in God despite adversity. But the answer is really an even greater mystery than that. In the suffering of Jesus, truly the most innocent of all men, we see the great love Christ has for us that He would offer Himself as the Lamb of God to die for us as an offering in penance and atonement for our sins. We also come to understand that the way to God is to be suffering servants, just as Jesus was. Jesus, as the new Adam, did not disobey God but rather lived his life as a suffering servant whose only thought was, *I come to do your will.* He and Mary remained obedient and faithful even in the midst of suffering, and they continued to love and serve God. In Jesus's suffering and in Mary's we can see the new Adam and Eve totally obedient to God, even through all the suffering and travails they endured while being wholly innocent.

"In the end, as in the story of Job, those who remain faithful and obedient through suffering can be redeemed if we offer our suffering to God in obedience. Through suffering, because it unites us with Jesus's suffering on the cross, we can go through a second baptism, the baptism of penance to wipe away sin. If we unite our suffering with Jesus's suffering on the cross, we can wash our souls clean in the blood of the Lamb of God, who takes away the sins of the world. In such a manner does God refine us, and as we learn from Isaiah, He has tested us in the furnace of affliction. The suffering we experience in this world makes us abandon our attachment to the world and turn to God. It brings us closer to Him who can deliver us and it helps us have compassion for the suffering of our neighbors. Through suffering, our souls are made to grow. It is God's great plan that we will become like Jesus and inherit the kingdom prepared from the foundation of the world as adopted sons and daughters. To be glorified with Him, we must suffer like Him so that we may recover by contrition and penance what we have lost by sin.

"I have seen much suffering. It can lead to ruin or to redemption. Recall that two thieves were crucified with Jesus. One thief let his suffering lead only to despair, while Jesus let His suffering lead to redemption, and the other thief repented and turned to Jesus to save him. The Romans meant Jesus's suffering for evil, but God meant it for good."

Susan had listened patiently. "I know, Sister. You're right. I know it in my soul. But it's hard. What do I do now?"

Sister continued to hold Susan's hands, and a slight smile came over her face as she looked into Susan's eyes. "You must trust in the great mercy of God, which is available to all who trust in Him, especially at three o'clock each day, the great hour of mercy, and maintain your focus. Search for the pearl of great price, and when you find it, give everything you have to acquire it."

"Where do I look, Sister? Where do I find it?"

"Recall the story of the finding of Jesus in the temple. Jesus told you where to look. He asked them why they were looking for Him. Did they not know that He must have been in His Father's house? You will find Him in His Father's house. Seek Him there, and you will find Him; knock, and it shall be opened for you. Whoever seeks, finds. Whoever knocks has the door opened. For the present, pick up your cross and carry it. Have faith, Susan, and pray the rosary, and the great Mother of God will ask Jesus to show you the way. I tell you the truth, more things are accomplished by prayer than this world dreams of. And remember: I am here for you always."

With that, the two survivors of John said goodbye and parted. John would remain with them always, and the years would not diminish their affection for him.

But there is still more to this story. Eugene Eckley, the assistant coach who had felt John was worth taking a chance upon, had fallen away from the church after his brother had been killed. He shook his fist at heaven and blamed God for not saving his brother, whom he considered a good man and whom he loved. But now, seeing the way John had lived and died, and after attending the funeral mass and hearing the words of Sister Francis, something changed him. He began to pray and repent and began attending church. Even in death John had returned the help Eugene had given him. The way John died changed how Eugene would live. In the end, the Lord gave to Job twice as much as he had before. He would do so again for Eugene, Susan, and John—two in this life and one in the next. To Him be all praise and glory, forever and ever!

ACKNOWLEDGMENTS

I owe thanks to the wonderful people who have influenced my life, including many whose names I cannot remember and who are known only to God. But I want to acknowledge my debt of thanks to them.

I also want to acknowledge and thank the sources that appear in the bibliography which, though not cited directly in the novel, have provided inspiration and helped inform its writing.

BIBLIOGRAPHY

De Rouville, Alexander.1985. *The Imitation of Mary: New Illustrated Edition*. Revised and Edited by Matthew J. O'Connell. New York: Catholic Book Publishing Co.

Kempis, Thomas A. *The Imitation of Christ*. 1983. ST PAULS, Homebush, Australia: ALBA HOUSE-Society of St Paul, New York.

Lang, J. Stephen. *Know the Words of Jesus in 30 Days*. 2010. New York: Guideposts.

Lang, Stephen. *Know the Bible in 30 Days*. 2008. New York: Guideposts.

Warren, Rick. *The Purpose Driven Life*. 2002. Grand Rapids, MI: Zondervan.

If I have inadvertently omitted or not given credit to any source, I sincerely apologize and would appreciate being notified.

Made in the USA
Las Vegas, NV
24 March 2021